The Frog Prince

Mike and Carl Gordon

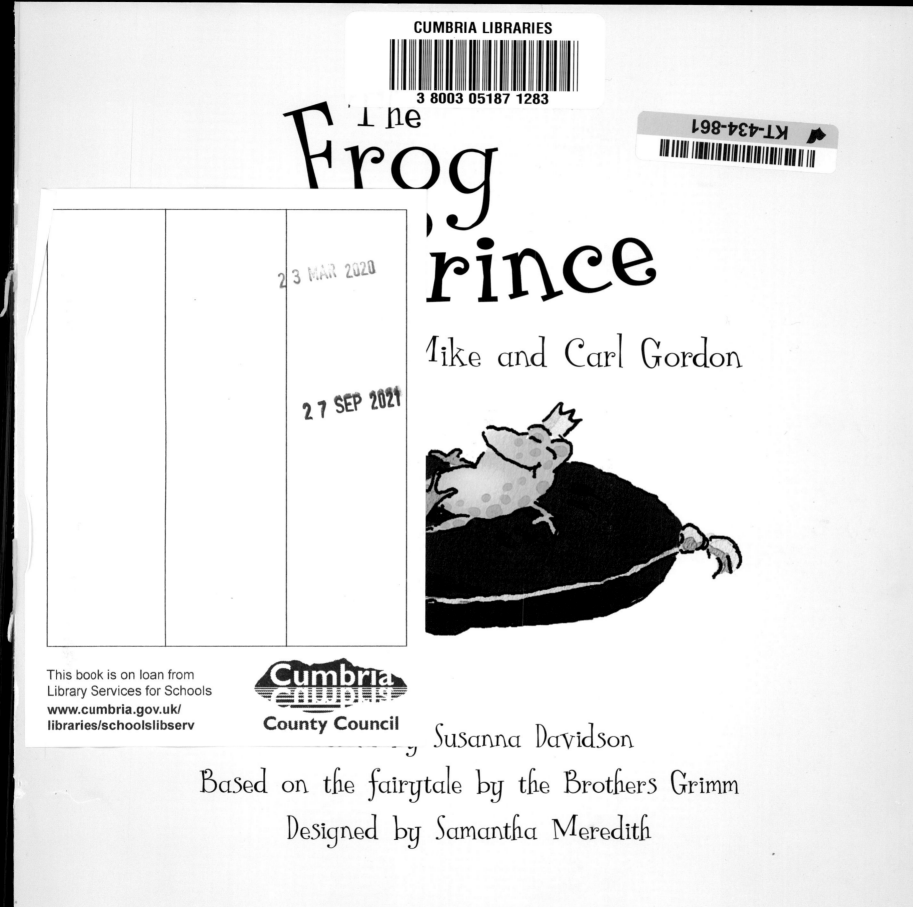

Retold by Susanna Davidson

Based on the fairytale by the Brothers Grimm

Designed by Samantha Meredith

Princess Poppy was furious. "I WON'T marry Prince Humperdink," she said.

"He's smelly and smug and slimier than a frog."

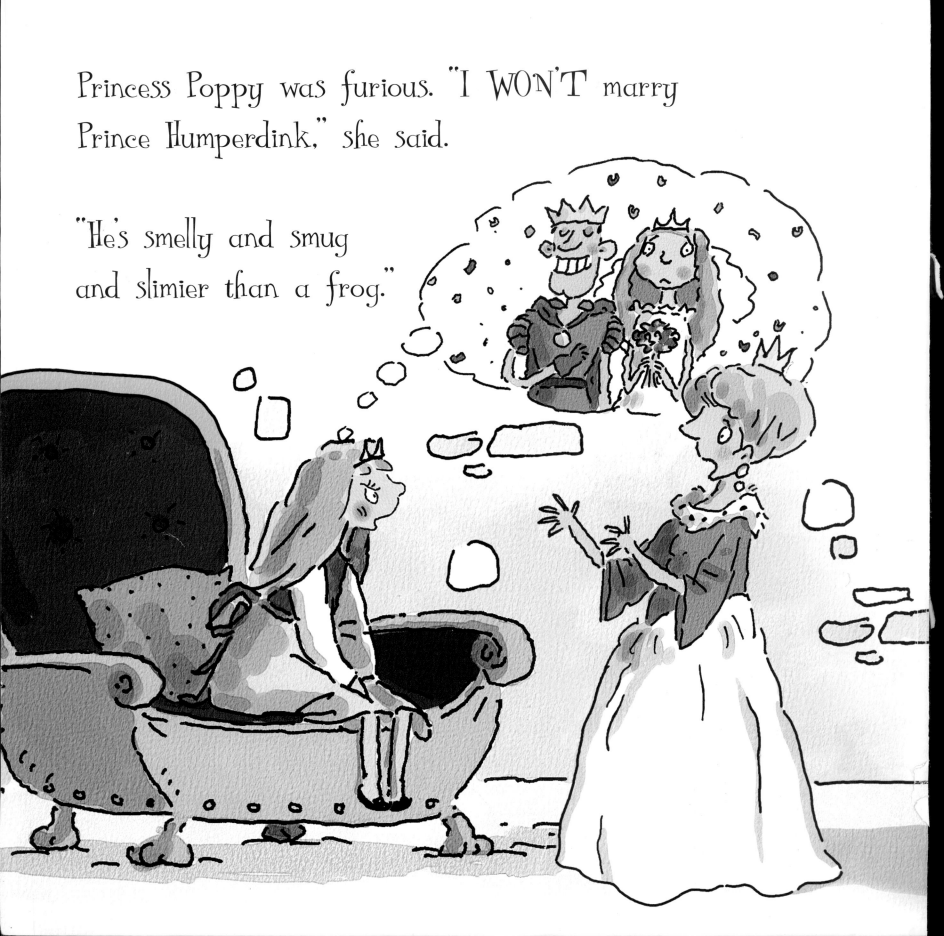

"You don't have to marry him now," said her mother.
"You just have to marry him when you grow up."

"I never want to marry him," said Poppy.
"I'd rather eat my toenails."

"I'll find another prince to marry," she snapped.

"You can have until tomorrow morning," said the King.
"But you'll never find a prince in that time."

"Just you wait," said Poppy.

And she stomped into the garden with her golden ball.

Poppy was so cross,
she didn't see the
wobbly stone.

She wibbled...

she wobbled...

She slipped and fell...

SPLAT!

...face-first into the pond.

Her golden ball plopped into the water.
"Help! I'm in big trouble now," wailed Poppy.

"Oh no you're not," croaked a frog.
"I can help you!"

"But in return..." said the frog.

"...I want to live in your palace, eat from your plate and sleep on your silken pillow."

"In your dreams," thought Poppy.

But out loud she said, "I promise."

As soon as the frog gave
Poppy her ball, she raced
back to the palace.

WAIT FoR me!

Poppy arrived just in time for dinner.
She had to sit next to Prince Humperdink,
who smelled of cabbage.

Then, to Poppy's horror, she heard a
splat... splat... splat...
In hopped the frog.

"Excuse me," said the frog.
"Princess Poppy promised I could stay with her."

"And princesses don't break promises,"
bellowed the King. "The frog is our guest."

"Thank you," said the frog, diving into Poppy's soup.

I don't think I'm hungry anymore.

"Now," said the frog, when he'd slurped up all the soup. "Time for bed."

"Oh no!" said Poppy. "You're not coming anywhere near my bedroom."

YOU CAN CARRY ME UP ON a CUSHION.

"Princesses don't break promises," repeated the King.

So Princess Poppy picked up the frog and dropped him in the darkest, most distant corner of her room...

"But Princess Poppy,"
said the frog, "you promised
I could sleep on your bed."

IF YOU DON'T LET ME,
I'LL TELL YOUR FATHER!

"I've had enough!" snapped Princess Poppy.
"You're the meanest, most horrible frog I've EVER met."

And with that, she threw
the frog out the window.

There was a long
silence, followed by
a loud **SPLAT**.

"Oh no!" thought Poppy.
"What have I done?"

She rushed outside
and picked up the frog,
as gently as she could.

"I'm so sorry," said Poppy.
And she bent down and kissed him.

There was a loud **CRASH**

and a deafening **BANG!**

In the place of the frog, stood a handsome prince.

"How can I ever thank you?" asked the Prince.
"Well," said Poppy, "you could marry me."

"Excuse me," said Prince Humperdink, "but Poppy is going to marry ME."

"Oh no I'm not," said Poppy.
"Daddy, you did say I could find my own prince...
and kings don't break promises either."

"That is true," sighed the King.

"In that case," said the Prince,
"Princess Poppy, will you marry me?"

"I will," said Princess Poppy.

And when she grew up she did...

...and they lived happily ever after.

Edited by Jenny Tyler and Lesley Sims

Digital manipulation by John Russell

This edition first published in 2011 by Usborne Publishing Ltd, 83-85 Saffron Hill, London EC1N 8RT, England.
www.usborne.com Copyright © 2011, 2007 Usborne Publishing Ltd. The name Usborne and the devices 🎈⊕ are Trade Marks
of Usborne Publishing Ltd. All rights reserved. No part of this publication may be reproduced, stored in a retrieval system,
or transmitted in any form or by any means, electronic, mechanical, photocopying, recording or otherwise,
without prior permission of the publisher. First published in America in 2011. UE.